BOOK
4

the NEW

crossing

The Case of the
Dinosaur in the Desert

Pauline Hutchens Wilson
Sandy Dengler

INTRODUCTION

It just isn't the same."

My dad sounded so sad. We stood on the walkway of a freeway overpass, looking out across a sea of new houses. Miles of houses, street after street.

"That line of trees out there is Sugar Creek." He waved an arm toward the hives of condos. "All this used to be farmland. When Paul Hutchens wrote those books about the Sugar Creek Gang, this is the area he wrote about. Right here."

I'm eleven, and, according to Dad, I'm older than most of the *homes* out here. "At least there's still a Sugar Creek," I said. "How far is it from our new place?"

"Couple miles. But the past—that was another world." He looked at me. "I'm sorry the fun is gone."

Dad walked down the slope to our car. I fell in behind him, wishing he didn't feel so sad.

When I was little, he read to me every night. And my favorite books to read were about a bunch of kids called the Sugar Creek Gang. They lived on farms near a creek and had a zillion adventures, mostly out in nature somewhere.

When Dad switched jobs, he found out we were going to move into the very area where

1

When lima beans explode in the microwave, it's not a pretty thing.

And it had started out as such a smooth, cool day, too. Dad was out of town at a lawyers' convention. Mom and the girls were gone for the evening, getting their hair done and hitting a back-to-school sale. And I, Les Walker, age eleven-plus, was baby-sitting myself for the first time ever. Unsupervised, as they say.

There were rules, of course. Aren't there always?

1. No guests.
2. Stay inside and keep the doors locked.
3. No cooking or baking.
4. And don't even think about touching my chemistry set.

Mom had dished my dinner out onto a plate and stuck it in the fridge— ground beef, carrots, and those huge, flat, tan lima beans that are called butter beans. All I had to do was lay a piece of waxed paper over the plateful and pop it in the microwave for two-and-a-half minutes.

OK, so I accidentally forgot the waxed paper step.

When some of the beans exploded, they

Sugar Creek County Park is a wee bit of nature stuck right in the middle of the residential area of the city. A chain-link fence separates that natural world from houses and lawns and an occasional pink plastic flamingo. As you walk the park's paths through woods and swamp, you see all kinds of creatures you wouldn't expect in town—turtles and frogs, raccoons and possums, and the most amazing birds. It's kind of like going back fifty years.

At the trail head on the east end is a picnic area. The grass is mowed, and massive wood-slab picnic tables under shady trees invite you to sit. That area is where the gang would meet.

I arrived first, and that was not usually the case. I'm not a real spry bird at 8:00 A.M. My dad sometimes teased me that people with red hair automatically sleep late, and—since mine is the reddest—I sleep in latest. But then, he'd also say that my freckles made me eat more. I learned fairly early not to believe every single thing he said.

Mike and Tiny arrived next. Tiny's name was really Clarence Wilson, and he was anything but tiny. He was very tall and gangling. He probably didn't weigh an ounce more than I did, and I didn't have enough meat to make a hot dog. He was all elbows when he walked. He carried binoculars almost all the time and probably knew every bird in America. Well, it seemed like it.

Mike Alvarado's grandparents came from Mexico, but you didn't hear any trace of an

"What was it?" Bits asked.

"Dinosaurs. And the rules said it couldn't be cartoony. It had to be as realistic as possible."

I interrupted. (I know, I shouldn't have.) "She drew these really neat raptors playing tag."

Lynn nodded. "That's what the judges liked, I guess. I read somewhere that play is a sign of intelligence in animals. And the raptors were supposed to be very intelligent dinosaurs. So I made them playing, and the judges caught on."

"What's the prize?" Mike's face looked as happy as if he were the winner himself.

"This is the great part! I get to go on a real dinosaur dig in Arizona, *and I can take some friends with me!*" She paused, looking from face to face. "Oh, come on, guys! You know it's you I'll take!"

I guess we should have cheered and yahooed more, but we just sat stunned. I'd expected the prize to be something like a hundred dollars or maybe a free dinosaur video. But to go on a real dig . . . all of us . . .

And then I guess it sank into all five of us at once, because we exploded like beans in a microwave. We sang, "We're going to Arizona! We're gonna dig dinosaurs!" Then we swarmed all over Lynn and picked her up like winning football players do to their coach.

But we didn't douse her with Gatorade.

university's budget allows just so much, you can't spend a penny more."

Tiny frowned. "In other words, you'd go, and one of us would go and three be left behind. Or maybe two could, and two couldn't."

Lynn nodded. She looked lower than a snake with a flat tire.

Mike shrugged. "So we draw straws. The winners go, and the losers don't."

Lynn shook her head. "I told them we're a . . . a . . . a close group. I forgot exactly how I said it. I said since we couldn't all go, I was declining. And I thanked them, of course."

"Oh, come on, Lynn!" Bits protested. "*You* can go. You won!"

"I know." That's all she said, but there was a bunch of meaning in it. She could go to Arizona and have a great time, but she didn't want to disappoint half the gang. I wasn't sure I could have done that, if it had been me.

"There's gotta be some way to work it out," I said.

Lynn half smiled. "That's what my father said. He was calling your father when I left. But rules are rules. Two people. Three, maybe. Not much you can do with that."

Tiny sucked in a bushel or so of air. "Well, let's go eat. The picture isn't going to look any rosier by starving ourselves to death."

I don't know if I mentioned it, but Tiny ate a lot.

So we locked our bikes to the bike rack and walked back the trail through the woods to the

Then we had just climbed down to the water's edge, trying to find where a bullfrog had disappeared to, when Mike stood erect. "Hey, quiet! Listen."

We froze and listened.

Lynn frowned. "Sounds like someone shouting for you, Les."

I could hear it, too. I scrambled back up to the trail and hollered as loud as I could. And I don't mind saying that when I really put some oomph into it, I can yell loud enough to call in airplanes.

The woods hung silent.

Then, very distant, came Dad's voice. "Les!"

"Yo!"

"He sounds like he's over on the main trail." Tiny waved an arm. "Les, you go back to the main trail. Mike and I will go on around to the end of the Loop—in case he's farther that way than we think."

I nodded and broke into a run back the way we had come. When Dad called out next time, he sounded closer. I reached the main trail and yelled again. In spite of all the trees and bushes and curves in the path, I found him pretty quickly.

Not him. Them. It was Dad and Mr. Wing, Lynn's dad.

Without an ounce of air to spare, I slowed to a walk. A stitch in my side didn't make talking any easier, either.

I stopped beside them and pointed to the cooler Dad carried. It was the red-and-white

Mr. Wing nodded to Dad. "You tell them." He was still busy with his ice cream.

Dad scraped his dish as he spoke. "Well, Mr. Wing and I discussed this problem about going on the dinosaur dig. We agreed that Lynn acted nobly, and we're both very proud of her."

I glanced at Lynn. She looked embarrassed.

"Now, Mr. Wing knows the ins and outs of colleges," Dad continued, "and he knew who to call. Pretty soon we worked out a deal with the university. We will pay for the transportation and provide for some cost-of-living expenses, and the university will cover what they have budgeted."

Lynn stared. "Does that mean . . ."

"It means that all five of you can go fry your weary little bodies in the Arizona sun, hunting dinosaurs."

a sleeping bag and pillow
towels and a washcloth
shampoo and soap (which I planned to use
    as little as possible)
a week's worth of clothes
a hat—the university insisted we bring
    broad-brimmed hats
a swimsuit
a flashlight
a compass to tell directions
binoculars
camp dishes and flatware
sunscreen
vitamins
not nearly enough money, I thought
and a whole lot of little odds and ends, like
    matches and a whistle

It was like going away to church camp, only with snakes.

Tiny, of course, had his bird book. From the library he also checked out a bunch of other field guides—on mammals, reptiles and amphibians, animal tracks, wildflowers, trees . . . If we didn't learn the name of every single thing we came across, it wasn't going to be his fault.

He thumbed through those books every chance he got. Every now and then he'd pipe up with, "Hey, look!" and spout off some weird bit of information as he pointed to a picture.

Time went so fast. There we were, trying to figure out what to take, and suddenly—bingo! —we were on our way.

The grass didn't grow up to the edge of the road anymore. The ground looked mostly bare except for rocks and small bushes. We passed very few trees, most of them small and down in gullies, which were nothing more than shallow creases in the land.

Even when the wind was blowing, the air hung hot most of the day. Our van was air conditioned, so when you got out at a rest stop, you really felt the outside heat.

We crossed from New Mexico into Arizona.

More cows. Many more cows. They stood around in the sparse shade of ragged little trees and high bushes.

The afternoon of the third day, Mr. Wing was driving. Dad navigated, shifting his attention between a road map and a sheet of written instructions.

Suddenly Dad waved an arm in the general direction of the left side of America. "Turn just ahead, and we should be there."

Nice theory, but I couldn't see any good place to turn. Here went an unpaved road off to the side, but that couldn't be it. The term "road" was giving it more class than it deserved. It was parallel tracks in the dirt, a pickup-truck-width apart. A gate closed it off. Gate? A loose tangle of barbed wire strung between two heavy sticks. The sticks were held to ragged wood fence posts by wire loops.

Dad slid out to open the gate. He pulled some wire loops off one of the big sticks and dragged the tangle of barbed wire aside. Mr.

4

My dad and Mr. Wing both claimed that, when they were growing up, they always wanted to be cowboys. I don't know why. They never lived on a ranch or even visited one that I knew of. I know I sure didn't yearn to ride around trying to outwit cows.

That is, until I met a real cowboy. Real cowboys are amazing.

The leader of the real cowboys now surrounding our van was a bulky, pot-bellied, jovial man with a bushy mustache. His battered black cowboy hat looked as if it had gotten the worst of seven hurricanes and a stampede. Maybe it had.

And the hats the other two wore weren't in much better shape. The other two, slim fellows, were probably from Mexico—or else their parents were. They frowned the whole time, watching us with distrust.

Dad rolled his window down and introduced himself, extending his hand. Hot, dry air poured in. It swamped the air conditioning instantly.

Still on his horse, the lead cowboy leaned forward in the saddle and reached out for the handshake. "Buck Barkley. So you all are with the university."

my teeth loose. I thought about the easy way those men rode. Horses slam up and down and sideways constantly when they move, but those riders didn't. They moved when the horses moved, and yet, their heads didn't go bobbing all over. Smooth. That was the word for it. Slick and smooth. Here I sat in a modern van with fancy suspension, and I was lurching around worse than those horsemen did.

A minute later, Tiny shrieked, "Stop!"

Mr. Wing slammed on the brakes. He must have thought a terrible accident was bearing down on us.

But Tiny, all excited, was peering out the window with his binoculars. "A desert sparrow! Black throat! See? That's a new one for my life list. I never saw one before!"

The very first time Tiny saw any particular bird species, he'd check it off on a printed sheet that listed every single bird in the United States. In a space by each one, he'd write down where and when he first saw it. That was his life list. I watched him put the date and place in tiny letters beside "Sparrow, black-throated."

He added two more birds to his life list before we completed those three miles to the research station.

"Research Station" has such an important-sounding ring to it. You expect half a dozen buildings the size of airline hangars, with a lot of trucks and equipment parked behind them. After all, a major university was running the thing.

no power out this far, so you run your fridge, lights, and air conditioning off a generator."

Bits wrinkled her nose. "And they sleep with that noise?"

Tiny dug out his desert-plants field guide. A few minutes later, he pointed to the bush Mr. Wing was sitting under and announced, "This is a creosote bush. *Larrea divaricata.*"

It's a poor day you don't learn something.

Dad looked at Mike. "You've been awfully quiet, Mike. Is anything wrong?"

Mike shook his head. "No. At least, I don't think so." He hesitated. "This afternoon when we met Mr. Barkley, remember?"

"Uh-huh."

"One of his cowboys said something in Spanish. I think he figured that it was safe— that you wouldn't know what he was saying."

"So what did he say?"

"That's what I wonder about. He asked, 'Do you think that these ones were sent out here to spy on us?' And Buck said, '*Tal vez,*'—maybe."

She ignored us five kids. She shook hands with Dad and Mr. Wing sort of automatically. "Dr. Alex Royer." She introduced her companion as Dr. Brian Fox.

She said welcoming words, but they didn't feel welcoming. Then she excused herself—something about pulling down her e-mail—and disappeared into the trailer with the pickle pails beside it.

The other paleontologist, Dr. Fox, still smiled warmly. "I don't remember names very well, but if you repeat them often enough, I'll catch on. Call me Brian." He looked at Lynn. "And you're Lynn, right? The artist."

Dad and Mr. Wing helped us unload our mountain of stuff and pile it on the ground under the creosote bush *(Larrea divaricata)*. Dr. Fox—I mean, Brian—helped, too. Dad went through the van to make sure we didn't leave something stashed under a seat or whatever.

Then Dad and Mr. Wing hugged us good-bye. They climbed back in the van. And there they went back out that rutted track, raising a big dust cloud, getting tinier and tinier.

I got the worst sad, sinking feeling as I watched them go. We were on our own in a dry desert wasteland.

Dr. Fox—I mean, Brian—stared at our mountain of stuff.

"Did we bring too much?" Tiny asked.

"Oh, we'll find somewhere to put it. Maybe stash some of it under a tarp outside. I see two tents. Can you kids put them up by yourselves?"

we tried to put up the tent. I must have put up our tent a dozen times when Dad and Mom and my sisters and I went camping. But always before, Dad or Mom would hand me the pieces and I'd stick them together. All of a sudden, I was dumping the storage bag out on the ground all by myself, and everything looked alike. It all looked wrong. No one handed me the piece that was supposed to come next.

It took Mike and Tiny and me half an hour to figure out how to do that five-minute job. When we finally got it all pegged and guyed right, we glanced over at the girls' tent site.

They were moved in already.

That night at dinner—canned beef stew, I think—Dr. Fox ate with us out at a picnic table.

Mike asked, "Doesn't Dr. Royer eat supper?"

Dr. Fox—Brian—nodded. "She's catching up on her reading—journals and papers. Besides, she usually doesn't eat beef. She prefers fresh vegetables. Carrots, cauliflower."

Blecch.

He talked about what they did. "In the movies, you'll see people using paintbrushes to dust off a perfect, articulated skeleton. It's not like that."

"Articulated means the bones are still the way they were when the animal died, right?" Tiny asked. "Sort of still together."

"Right. Head still connected to neck, neck still connected to spinal column. It all looks very dramatic on film. The reality is, most dinosaurs' parachutes failed to open."

"Mark the place. Then come tell one of us." He showed us other samples, explaining what we should look for.

Finally it was bedtime. From the little storage shed, Brian dragged out five cots. He said he didn't want us to sleep on the ground. I figured it was so we'd be comfortable, but then he casually added, "Lot of snakes out here."

I was sure glad Mom couldn't hear him.

The girls slept inside their tent, but Mike, Tiny, and I had to set up our cots outside. No room in our tent—our stuff filled it.

I didn't get much rest. You know how you never sleep well the first night.

I stared up at the bezillion stars. You see more stars out on the desert where city lights don't blot them out. Millions more. I spent a lot of time listening to soft, weird noises. Wondering what was making those sounds out there. Feeling the brush of strangely dry, warm air on my cheeks.

And wishing Dad hadn't driven away.

and bossed Brian around as if he were one of us kids. She didn't say anything friendly. Not even a please or thank you.

Dr. Royer spent most of her time working on part of a warped and flattened skull buried in soft rock. I wouldn't have known what it was if Brian hadn't told us.

We Creekers were assigned to dig out a large flat bone from a dinosaur shoulder.

First we had to dig away the overburden— that was the dirt on top of the rock layer the fossil was in. That pickax work was fun for about five minutes. From then on it was hard labor. Then we had to dig all around the bone, using hammers, ice picks, and chisels to chip away at the soft, gritty matrix. Matrix was the rock the bone was buried in.

We couldn't dig too close to the fossil, either, because it was softer and more brittle than the rock around it. I wondered how you got rid of all the rock if it was harder than the fossil, but I didn't ask out loud. I suppose I should have, but I was afraid that Dr. Royer would call me stupid or get mad. She had already made fun of Mike once when he asked a question.

We stopped for lunch about ten. That part was neat. I'm always ready to stop for lunch. I loved the cooking: sandwiches and what Mom would certainly call "junk food"—potato chips. You can't do better than that.

After lunch, we chipped at the fossil some more. By now, still buried in its block of grainy out exploring a little. Tiny, Lynn, and Mike headed off in another direction. We took our potato chips along because we hadn't eaten them yet. I also took my new compass and wrote down which direction we were heading. Just to be safe.

After a couple hundred yards, I looked back downhill. The dig showed up as a white scar on the side of a low rise. We walked up the slope through crunchy gravel and no grass at all. Some of the short bushes looked dead. But at lunch Brian had said they were only dormant and they'd leaf out again when it rained.

When we reached the top of the little hill, we looked down on a broad, flat, white valley. Beyond it, ragged-looking gray mountains jutted up.

"Cool," I said.

"It's a hundred degrees!" Bits snapped.

"Not that kind of cool, and you know it. I'm sure glad Tiny isn't with us." I led the way downhill a short distance. I was headed for an outcrop of rounded tan rocks jutting out of the hillside.

She followed. "Why?"

"We'd never get this far. We'd only be fifty feet from the dig, waiting while he looked up stuff." I picked out a low, flat rock and sat down. My head was all sweaty under my hat.

She giggled as she sat on a crumbly rock beside mine. She looked out across the flat valley awhile. "I wonder how they knew to dig in that particular place. I mean, look how much

Did I hear horse hooves? I got up straight on my knees. "Hey, look! Someone's out there."

A distant horseman had just come into view around the side of our hill, down near the flats.

Bits peered into the hot sunlight. "It looks like Mr. Barkley. I mean Buck. Hey, maybe he knows what this is."

"Yeah!" So we ran down the hill, yelling.

He saw us and turned his horse up the hill to meet us. He reined in beside us. "Well, look who's here. Lost?"

"No, sir. I mean no, Buck. We're just out messing around." Bits handed him the black stone. "Do you know what this is?"

He grinned. "That's a tenontosaur tooth." He said it teh-NON-t'sore. "They were thirty feet long, ate grass."

"Dinosaurs?"

"Yep. Kind of a duckbill. Common around here. Where'd you find it?"

So we ran back up to the outcrop, with him right behind us. I showed him the exact place on the slope where I'd picked it up.

He grinned. I knew because his bulky mustache moved, not because we could see his hidden mouth. "And hit looks like you got a nice piece of jaw sticking out right there." He pointed.

"Oh, wow!" I hadn't even noticed that big gray-brown streak. Now that I knew what it was, it even looked like a lower jaw. And when we got down close we could see a couple of teeth in it, all gritty and gray.

He made sure again that we weren't lost,

7

I didn't notice the burning heat a bit as we ran with our tooth back over the hill to the dig. We hollered to Brian when we were still halfway up the hill.

He came running toward us, looking panicked. I guess he assumed something was wrong. I didn't think we'd been yelling that loud.

"Look!" I dropped our precious find into his hand.

He grinned. "Tenontosaur tooth! Great! Can you go back to the spot?"

You bet we could! He made us each take a long drink of water first. Then we three headed straight up the hill.

We must have climbed the hill in a different place this time, though. When we got to the top, it didn't look exactly right. We couldn't just pick out our outcrop; a lot of the same sort of rocks stuck out all around. Hundreds of the same sorry little bushes hunched over in the hot sun.

But all we really had to do was find my hat. It took fifteen minutes at least before Brian suddenly pointed and said, "Over there!"

A word of warning: Don't wear a light tan hat out in the desert. It's the same color as the ground. My hat was really hard to see. It lay a ming on the bottom of the pail that I remembered the reason we slept off the ground on cots. Rattlesnakes and scorpions. By then I was out there, so I didn't have any choice but to walk back through a dark minefield full of nasty things waiting to bite or sting me. I walked very carefully, a step at a time, listening for rustles or buzzes.

What I heard, though, was Dr. Royer talking to Brian Fox.

I repeat, I didn't mean to listen in, but her voice carried loudly on the night air. She was saying, "This has gone far enough, Brian. I want them out!"

His soft voice purred, "You don't know that they stole those tools. It could be . . ."

"Who else would? They're the only volunteers here now. And they could hide a horse in that mountain of trash they hauled in here!"

"Frankly, Alex, I don't think we have any say in the matter."

"I know!" Her voice rose sharply. "And that infuriates me. It absolutely infuriates me! The dean obligated me to baby-sit these rowdy children without consulting me. No one asked me if I wanted to do this. They simply promised the winner that he could come dig with me. He or she. Apparently, even though it's my dig, my consent wasn't necessary."

"But it's not the kids' fault. And their parents went to additional expense to make it happen for all of them."

"That's another thing! The contest was sup-

8

Mike Alvarado was just one surprise after another. At ten, he was a year younger than the rest of us and small for his age. But until we came on this expedition, he had been doing grown-up work, helping his brothers in their lawn service. He spent long hours every day mowing, raking, and trimming.

Now I saw a whole new side of him I'd never seen before.

The next morning, Dr. Royer, Brian, and the five of us Creekers started up the hill to find the spot where we'd found the tooth.

And Mike, goofy little Mike, said, "Let me try something, OK? Stay behind me so you don't trample the ground, and I'll try to track them."

I was saying, *Oh, yeah, sure,* to myself. And Bits said exactly that out loud.

Mike didn't pay any attention to her. In that half-light before dawn, he began walking across the hill a little way out above the dig. Suddenly he stopped, peered closer, and then started up the slope at kind of an angle.

We followed.

I pointed. "Hey, Bits, there's where you picked up that pink-streaked rock."

"I hope you're not falling for this story. Surely you don't really believe this little grade-school urchin can follow tracks. It's a show, so we won't suspect them."

Mike looked near tears. "My grandpa, he's a great tracker. Poppa says he can track a soaring eagle back to the egg it hatched from. And he showed my brothers and me how."

"Do tell." She could really pile on the sarcasm with only two words. "You're out! That's it. And believe me, all your belongings will be thoroughly searched. You are not leaving here with one little bit of anything that doesn't belong to you!" And she marched away over the hill.

I'd been yelled at a lot in my eleven years, but nobody had ever lit into me that loudly or that angrily before. And usually, if someone yelled at me, I at least partway deserved it. I was so stunned I couldn't think of anything to say or do. I just stood there with my mouth hanging open. I probably looked about as intelligent as your average fence post.

Brian looked embarrassed.

Bits looked howling mad. "We didn't do that! I don't know who dug around here, but it wasn't us!"

A few feet away, Tiny asked, "Les? This yours?" He was holding up my potato chip bag.

"Yeah! I forgot about them. I didn't even get to eat them."

Tiny walked over and handed the bag to Brian. "Well, it's empty now. I'm wondering if

same spot on earth all the time—and there are enough of them that you can probably hit a couple from just about anywhere in the world.

While Brian got a position reading, the rest of us searched for more fossils, but we didn't find any.

When we got back to camp, Dr. Royer began tossing our stuff into the back of the crew cab. She wasn't being very gentle, either.

She snarled, "I've arranged for security to meet you at the university to make certain you don't have anything that's not yours. Brian, strike their tents and take them back to town." She glared right at Lynn. "And I never want to see them again."

chunk of material. He went off to make some phone calls while we waited for our food.

Bits leaned forward, elbows on the table. "Les, you gotta get hold of your dad. Maybe he can threaten some kind of legal thing and make Dr. Royer back down."

Tiny nodded. "Or Lynn's dad. He knows his way around a university."

Lynn sighed. "I feel so terrible. I started all this. I wish I'd never sent that picture in."

"Hey, is not your fault!" Mike grinned. "It's an adventure, OK? Where we go don't matter much. This is fun right here, this motel, right? Did you see that swimming pool? Let's just do all we can and enjoy all we can. You people wanna go mope, you go mope. Me, I'm gonna have fun."

Lynn forced a smile. "He does have a point."

Here came our lunches. Brian showed up a minute later.

I was too hungry to chat. I ate. And while I ate, I thought about Mike's attitude. It was a great attitude. And yet, getting accused of stealing and being yelled at ripped me up inside more than I wanted to admit.

As I stood in line at the cash register, I calculated how much money it would cost just for food if we stayed here for, say, three days. If breakfast cost less and dinner cost more, lunch was about the middle. Three times this check each day for three days was nine times this check. I really hadn't brought enough money!

Brian said he'd see what he could do and

"And Paul in Romans. Just a minute. I'm looking for it."

Now, notice here, when Dad said, "Just a minute," he was talking about a cell phone minute that was costing him money. That shows you right there how serious he was.

Dad is memorizing-impaired. Always has been, always will be. He cannot memorize worth beans, especially the numbers for chapters and verses in the Bible. And yet, he knows the Bible better than just about anyone else I know. He can tell you what it says, and he can find it and show it to you. He just can't memorize it.

His voice came on again. "Here it is. Romans 12:18. 'If it's possible, as much as lies in you'—that is, as much as you can—'live peaceably with all.' Next verse: 'Don't avenge yourself but rather give place to wrath: for it is written, Vengeance is mine; I will repay, says the Lord.' I've also seen that translated as 'Never avenge yourself, but leave room for the wrath of God.'"

I know Dad was reading out of the King James Bible because that has always been his favorite. But when he would read to me, he'd make some of the words more modern. That way it sounded more like it was for me and not just for someone four hundred years ago.

He wasn't done yet. "And here's the kicker, Les. Verse 20: 'Therefore if your enemy hungers, feed him; if he thirsts, give him drink: for in so doing you will heap coals of fire on his head. Be not overcome of evil, but overcome evil with good.'"

"Twelve, I think. I'm not sure."

She found it, exactly what Dad had read, and read it off to us. She started up higher than Dad did, though—she read the whole chapter.

When she finished, we all just sat there while the silence got thicker and thicker.

Finally Lynn said, "Pretty clear instructions."

Bits wagged her head. "I don't think I can do that."

Tiny was staring a big hole in the floor. "OK, so let's say that Dr. Royer is an enemy. A genuine enemy."

"I'd say that." Bits's voice dripped sarcasm.

"Here we sit in town, and our enemy is out in the boonies on the dig site. So there's nothing we can do. The way I see it, God is going to have to either bring her here or send us out there."

"Yeah." I could see what he meant. "Unless God does something, there's no contact. So you're saying that the next move is God's."

Finally, a plump, grandmotherly woman with gray hair came out and extended her hand. "My name is Margaret Brewer," she said. Brian shook hands with her and introduced two of us—he remembered Lynn's name and Mike's. So Bits and Tiny and I introduced ourselves.

The secretary brought more chairs into the woman's office. Between the extra chairs and a sofa along one wall, we all found a seat.

We talked awhile. Rather, she asked questions, and we answered them. The usual stuff—where we went to school, what we liked about the town we lived in, what we wanted to be when we grew up.

Then Brian explained everything that had happened so far.

Dr. Brewer sat back in her huge, leather-covered, padded chair. She propped her elbows on the chair arms, her fingertips together in a tent shape.

When he finished, she thought a moment, her lips pushed out. Finally, she said, "We certainly don't want to look like an institution that does not honor promises or reward exceptional students. We can't run a contest and then yank away the prize. As far as I'm concerned, Lynn here—and one friend, at least—must be allowed to continue, as agreed upon."

"Margaret, they're all five good workers. They dug out a hefty chunk and jacketed it in a day and a half. Adult volunteers sometimes don't do that well. I agree regarding the pub-

11

Right after our meeting with Dr. Brewer, we changed into play clothes and clambered back into Brian's truck. He took us to an aged brick building at the far end of the school.

I got surprised again. In an old book about dinosaurs, the pictures of the laboratories showed huge rooms with men in white coats varnishing beautiful dinosaur skeletons. Not here.

The paleo preparation lab we went into was a long, narrow room. Wooden tables stretched for the length of the room, and they were cluttered with things people were working on. The chairs looked like stuff you retrieve from the dump. But to me, that didn't detract a bit. It all felt comfortable and well used and loved and homey. You could almost feel that the people who worked there really enjoyed what they were doing.

Along one wall, steel shelves held labeled boxes. The labels said things like "dental picks, 1" chip brushes, chisels, pin vises, X-acto knives, files, wire" . . . a hundred strange things, and I didn't have the slightest idea what any of them might be used for here.

Brian stood in the middle of the floor beside a table. "Any one of you ever make miniatures? You know—dollhouses, ships, cars?"

you still remember where it goes." He put the broken chip back on with plain old superglue.

Then he stood up. "Let's go look at some bone that's been prepped out, so that you know what it looks like when it's cleaned." He took us to a huge room with lots and lots of metal cases taller than Dad.

He opened the double doors of a case. It was full of huge steel drawers. He pulled open a drawer. It was obviously extremely heavy, and that figures—it was full of rocks. Each rock, though, was a dinosaur bone, lying on padding.

"Wow!" all five of us said at once.

The cleaned fossils were darker and smoother than stuff right out of the ground. You could even tell what some were. I recognized ribs. And a pointy bone a little bigger than my hand was obviously the last bone of a toe. Once upon a time, a giant creature walked with that toe and maybe even stubbed it on a rock or something.

Then we went back to the lab. Brian was a good teacher. In no time at all, we had the hang of it. He showed us how to use an airscribe, a noisy little pen-size jackhammer that you hold the way you'd hold a pencil to draw. It cuts away matrix in a hurry.

Then he took Lynn and me to the other end of the room and showed us how to make rubber molds and plaster casts of fossils. It's too much to explain, but I will say that they use regular old white modeling clay to set up the molds. And they use toilet paper for every-

Mike bubbled. "A really neat one, with a low dive!"

"Then we'd better shut down here. Any of you have to buy a swimsuit? We'll stop by a store if you do."

Now that was plain old thoughtful! But we were church-camp pros, and we knew you never go camping without a swimsuit.

In came an older woman. I recognized her: Dr. Margaret Brewer, the nice bigwig whose office had the fish tank and potted palms. She smiled cheerfully. "How's it going?"

Brian said, "Great!" even as Bits complained, "Terrible! Look at this!" She waved a hand across the jacket with its fossil. "We worked on this all day and didn't get anywhere!"

Dr. Brewer wandered over and studied it a moment. "How far along was it when you began work on it?"

Brian said, "We took the lid off this morning."

She raised her eyebrows. "I see what you mean about their being good workers. They accomplished quite a lot in only one day."

Quite a lot? As Bits said, it looked as if we hadn't gotten anywhere. There was so much still untouched. You would think, with five people chipping away at it all day, it would be about done. I once heard someone say that the tyrannosaur skeleton called Sue would take a million hours to prep. I was beginning to see how slow that kind of work really is.

"And that's not all!" Brian bragged. He led her to the far end of the room. He showed her

12

We had a good time in the pool when we got back to the motel. We would have had a lot better time—at least, a longer time—if some guy hadn't come out and said we weren't allowed to be there without an adult supervisor. So we went back to our rooms and got dressed.

When Brian took us to dinner at a fast-food place, we didn't mention about the pool. We'd be leaving in the morning anyway, and we didn't want him to feel bad.

He took us back after supper. We were going in the side door when a soccer ball came bouncing past us. Three Mexican-looking boys our age were playing a pickup game in the empty back parking lot. You can't get very serious about a game when there are only three.

I don't know how Mike does it. One minute he was headed in the side door, and the next minute he was kicking the ball back to them and running after it. And a minute after that, all five of us were on the "field," if that's what you can call a burning-hot parking lot.

It would be three against five, so Mike played on their side. The goals were a trash bin at one end of the lot and a Dumpster at the other. After a while we stopped to catch our

Nope. Brian got us up and going long before dawn cracked, and I slept in the backseat of the pickup nearly all the way.

I woke up a few minutes before we pulled into the yard at the camp. I could tell we were "home." The generator was hammering away behind the bushes. Now that I was used to it, it sounded reassuring. The world is still modern, its constant rattle promised.

Standing on her cement-block porch, Dr. Royer watched us pull up in front of her trailer. She was not happy, and she didn't seem to mind a bit letting us know that. She didn't say hello or even look at us. "Take them out to V 16. They can pitch their tents and unload this evening."

"Let me put the fresh stuff in the fridge." Brian went to the back of the truck for the bags of milk and lettuce and things.

Bits and I were closest to the doors, so we hopped out and helped him so that he would have to make only one trip. Because, you see, we had a plan.

The plan was this. We were going to be so supernice to Dr. Royer that she'd feel ashamed for yelling at us. No matter how ugly she would get, we would stay pleasant. We would be extra-helpful. We would pray for her—out loud when possible. We would heap on "coals of fire." We would kill our enemy with kindness.

As Brian and Bits and I came out of the trailer to get back into the pickup, a ratty old truck came chugging into the yard. It was all

For once I remembered to pray *before* instead of after. Without bowing my head or anything, I asked God to let us know what He wanted us to do and to work it out His way.

It didn't take but a minute or two to sort out that Lynn and Tiny would stay. Mike, Bits, and I would go with Buck. When he said we'd be back in a couple of days, Dr. Royer said, "Don't hurry."

We dragged everything out of the back of Brian's pickup. We left the tents for Lynn and Tiny. We gathered up our sleeping bags and toothbrushes and underwear. We dumped our stuff into the back of Buck's truck. Instantly, Bits and Mike clambered up into the bed. I climbed in behind them.

As we went lurching and pitching out of the yard, we waved good-bye to Lynn and Tiny and Brian. And I thought how much Dad liked cowboy things, and how he would just love a chance like this to actually do cowboy work.

Then we couldn't see the research station anymore, partly because we were down around a hill and also because the dust cloud boiling up behind us was too thick to see through.

I had asked God to work it the way He wanted, so this must be what He wanted. He was sending us off to be cowboys!

about keeping horse and cow droppings cleaned up, either. On the other hand, I could see that when the manure dried out enough, it sort of bleached and broke up into powder. Eventually it looked like the dirt. So how much of this dusty ranch yard, I wondered, had once passed through the gut of a large plant-eating animal?

Buck waved an arm toward a long, narrow building with windows. "You boys can stash your bedrolls in the bunkhouse there. Missy, you can sleep in the cook's shed over there. Hit's separate and safe."

A real cowboy bunkhouse! What I wouldn't give for Dad to be here now, to join us and live out his dream.

It was way past lunchtime, and I was hungry. Buck didn't seem to notice the time, and Bits and Mike didn't mention anything, so I didn't, either. Mike and I piled our stuff on lumpy beds in the bunkhouse and went back to the truck. Buck had just loaded two big water cans with faucets at their bottoms.

He dipped his head toward the house. "Come on in. I gotta get your addresses and phone numbers and stuff. Don't suppose you kids have picture ID of some sort. Or a passport. Jest in case INS comes calling."

"Our school issues photo IDs," Bits said, "but I didn't bring mine."

And we followed him off to the house.

"Who's I and S?" I asked.

"Immigration and Naturalization Service,"

the ocean. So did the little trilobite fossils there. He had filled an Indian basket with fossil teeth from deinonychus and tenontosaurs. He had some big triangular shark teeth.

He also had a huge rattlesnake skin. It was nailed to a long board. And I do mean long—almost the whole length of the mantel! The rattles were still attached, which is how I knew it was a rattler. Wouldn't Tiny love to see this thing!

Then Buck wrote down my full name, address, phone number, and citizenship.

I volunteered, "And my e-mail address is . . ."

"Don't need it. I don't do that fancy computer stuff. What's your daddy's name?"

"William."

"Same address?"

"Yes, sir. I mean, Buck." That puzzled me for a minute. Of course he'd have the same address. And then I realized that no, maybe he wouldn't. A lot of kids' fathers don't live with their mothers.

Finally Buck had as much info as he wanted to get. The paperwork was done. We were ready to become cowboys.

reddish brown with white faces. A couple of them were dark brown and brindled. And you could smell them. That surprised me. But the only way I was used to seeing cows was out a car window or on a CD-ROM. You can't smell them that way. It was a strange smell, sweet in a way.

Buck parked by the trees, and we jumped down out of the truck bed.

"You kids ride much?" he asked.

"Yeah! My uncle had horses," Mike crowed. "But I only rode in the corral."

Bits offered, "Lynn and I took riding lessons one summer. We rode in circles around an indoor arena."

"Well, don't worry. You'll catch on right away. Ain't nothin' to it." Buck waved an arm toward the trees. "Manny! Take these three over to the remuda and outfit 'em."

I always thought the word *remuda*—which is a bunch of horses—was pronounced reem-YOU-duh, with a Y in it somewhere. Buck pronounced it ree-MOO-duh. I envied the way he could just slip in and out between English and Spanish, as if they were all one language.

We followed the slim, Mexican man named Manny over to a kind of crease in the hillside. Crowded into that little draw were five horses. The cowboys had strung rope from tree to tree and bush to bush, making a floppy sort of holding pen. If the horses simply started walking, they could have walked right through it. But they didn't seem inclined to move. They had a good point. Man, was it hot!

blue-white eyes, but he didn't try to move away. I wrapped the lead rope around his neck. When I pulled, he came along. I don't know what I would've done if he decided to stay standing still.

I noticed as I led him over to Manny and Mike (who had caught a pretty little brown-and-white pinto) that Buck had left. I guess when you're the boss, you don't have to work in the heat.

Manny taught us how to bridle and saddle our horses. He showed us how to neck-rein them to change directions, how to start them and stop them. Stopping my particular horse was not a problem. He loved to quit. Making him go was a chore.

Bits's horse didn't want to do what she told him to do. Manny said to her, "Don't be afraid to make him shape up. You're not strong enough to hurt him. Take him out to those mesquites out there," and he pointed toward some big scrubby bushes.

Bits's horse didn't want to leave the others. But she wrenched his head around and thumped her heels in his ribs, over and over. She wasn't cruel, but she sure was firm. He walked clear out to the trees whether he wanted to or not. And I got the message that I was going to have to be boss of my horse, too.

That afternoon we became true cowboys.

As the sun dropped lower, Manny and the other fellow, Roberto, saddled up and climbed aboard. Whistling and yelling and swinging stuff

Sounds crazy, I know. But without the discomfort, it wouldn't have been as much fun.

As we rode mile upon mile, I thought of times in the past when I complained about being uncomfortable or hot or whatever. And I realized that the less-than-comfortable is as much a part of God's gift as is the comfort. To appreciate the gift best, you have to experience all of it.

By the time we reached the ranch, I was getting a little stiff, but I'd expected that. This was new, this riding a horse for hours. We ate beef stew that night in a big dining room, and we slept in a real bunkhouse.

I ask you: Could it get any better than this?

And if she had half a head on, she'd pay regular hired help. Plenty of people around wanting the work. She'd get her fossils dug up, and she wouldn't be all that much out of pocket, either. More coffee, any of you?"

We muttered something along the lines of, "No, thank you." We weren't a very cheery bunch.

Buck and his cowboys chatted in Spanish awhile. I glanced at Mike now and then, but he didn't look as if he knew what they were saying.

Then Buck stood and clapped his hands. "Let's saddle up!"

Bits groaned, and Mike let his face drop forward into his empty plate.

Out we staggered, down to the barn.

I remembered pretty well the lessons I'd learned the day before. I put the saddle on my horse correctly. Roberto had to tighten it. We weren't strong enough to draw the cinches up safely.

Bits's horse didn't want to let her put the bit in its mouth. She gave it a wrench the way Manny had shown her, and it slipped right in. She was sure enjoying this horse business, pain or not. She climbed aboard before either Mike or I got going.

We swung the big corral gates open. The cows didn't want to leave. Manny and I rode into the corral and around the back side, sticking close to the fence. Then Manny whooped and swung his reins. I tried to whoop the same way, but I hurt too much to swing anything.

The cows milled around. Then a couple of

horse aside and just let the cattle go where they wanted. Their dewlaps—those loose flaps of skin under their necks— flopping, they walked and then jogged up over a rise. They threaded among tall saguaro cactus and some nasty five-foot-high cactus called chollas. Why they never got stickers, I have no idea.

I made my horse jog over to Manny. "Where are they going?"

"They smelled water. A *tinaja* over the rise there."

"What's a tee-NAH-hah?"

"A low spot or a dip in the rocks where water collects. Just runoff water. Cows can smell water for miles if they're thirsty enough."

"Wow!"

He twisted in his saddle and waved an arm toward a low hill to the south of us. "That low rise is the back side of Plug Horse mesa. So we took 'em as far as we need to. They found the water, and they'll find the grass. Lotsa grass up there. We can head back."

I nodded. "I been thinking about that. As far as we rode away from the ranch, we gotta ride that far back again."

Manny grinned. "No, you don't." He gave his horse a thump. It lurched into a rocking-horse canter, back the way we came.

My horse took off at a canter right after it and almost dumped me. I hung on and just let him go. Why would I want to stop him? It was the fastest he'd moved since I met him.

angled down onto a two-rut track that probably thought itself a road. Then he could go a little faster, but not much.

When we rattled into the ranch yard, our horses were standing in a corner of the corral by the water trough. The gate was still wide open. Bits's sorrel was lipping some hay in a manger. The others dozed, their noses drooping. I have never figured out how horses sleep on their feet like that.

Still another surprise in a day full of surprises: Brian Fox's Jeep was parked by the ranch house. He and Tiny and Lynn were sitting under a tree. They stood up as we came into the yard. They walked up to our truck the moment it stopped.

Lynn didn't even say hello, and that's not like her. "I'm so glad you guys are back. We need you."

help. We made a big find, and we only have a week to get it out."

"Why only a week?" Bits asked. She scrunched up in the corner of a wicker sofa.

"Dr. Royer has to go back and teach a summer class."

We sat there in silence a few moments. I didn't know about the others, but I was simply cooling off. Between the soft mist and the ice, I was beginning to realize how hot I'd been for the last few days.

Bits scratched her head. We all needed shampoo. "Lynn . . ." She hesitated. "I don't know how to say this except to just say it. I'm having too much fun here. Riding horses all day. I don't want to go back."

Mike bobbed his head. "It's so neat, Lynn! We got the whole desert to ride in. It's not like back home, or at my uncle's. And we're doing real stuff."

Lynn looked worried. "You do real stuff at the dig."

"But this is different!"

I glanced at Tiny. He was scowling at the worn boards in the porch floor. When he looked like that, it meant he was thinking.

Lynn protested, "You guys came out here to dig dinosaurs, not chase cows around!"

Bits got louder. "Lynn, stop and think! Horses! We get to ride horses. I mean really ride them, not just mess around with them. Don't you remember? When we were going around that boring old riding arena, we used to talk

When it looked like we'd get sent home again, things turned right around. I think these are signs that the dig is where the Lord wants us to be. He got us there. You might say He went out of His way to get us there."

Mike grumped, "Yeah, but—"

Tiny pressed on. "No buts about it. He got us there. It isn't near as much fun to stick to the plan as it is to gallop all over on horses, but we said we would do it. We sort of made a promise—gave our word—to God and to each other. I think we ought to keep it."

"But, Tiny . . ." Bits whined. When she whined, it meant things were going against her. "That was before Buck's offer. God can't hold us to a promise we made before we found out we can work here instead of at the dig."

"Sure He can. I can. And I've always been proud that I keep my word. I'm going to work for Dr. Royer and follow the plan the best I can."

Bits turned to me. "Les, talk sense into him! You like riding horses as much as I do. I can tell."

She was right. This being genuine cowboys on a genuine ranch was great. I felt terribly torn inside while what I liked better fought it out with what I really ought to be doing.

And I might as well mention that it's a battle that goes on inside me pretty often. Sometimes I stick with what's right and sometimes . . . but anyway, here I was tussling with myself again.

just stick with our plan. After all, we based it on His Book."

Buck started arguing about what a lousy person Dr. Royer was and that we were foolish to try to help her. He said she'd hate us just as bad after we did her work as she did now.

And Brian asked, "What plan?"

the hundred feet up to the dig. Then we went back for the tools and other stuff.

Mike grumbled, "I sure wish we could just leave this stuff here overnight, 'stead of dragging it all around every day."

I swung my backpack over one shoulder and picked up Mike's and Lynn's. "Yeah, and V 20 is even farther up its hill. But Brian said stuff keeps disappearing if you don't put it away or lock it up. He said more tools turned up missing after Dr. Royer called us thieves and sent us away."

"Oh, I see." Lynn gathered up the pickax and shovel. "Since things were stolen when we weren't there, she couldn't use that as an excuse to keep us away."

Mike brought the big canvas bag with the ice picks, geology hammers, rolls of toilet paper, and stuff. See? I told you paleontologists use toilet paper all the time. When you're using it on a dig or in the lab, though, you call it paleo paper.

We trudged up the hill, loaded like pack mules. First, we would set up the shade frame. Mike unfolded the blue tarp and dragged it across our dig. Then he tossed the poles, one to each corner of the tarp.

When I reached for a pole lying beside the tarp, the ground squirmed.

I froze.

Again, the dirt beside the pole rearranged itself.

Lynn claimed later that I yelled, jumped

"I never realized they're so beautiful!" Lynn purred. Only Lynn would call a rattler beautiful. But she was right. It was, in a weird, twisted way.

Mike said, "You know why Manny and Roberto and Buck wear them guns and holsters? To shoot coyotes and rattlers. Manny told me so. Wish we had a gun now."

Lynn gasped. "That's terrible. My dad says coyotes aren't bad! They're valuable to farmers and ranchers. They eat mice and rabbits and other animals that eat grass and grain—the food the cows and horses are supposed to be eating. So the smart rancher *wants* coyotes. And it's not right to kill snakes, either. Rattlesnakes are becoming endangered."

"Hey, don't tell me. I just tell you what Manny said." Mike moved back a step, still watching the snake. "So what we gonna do, Miss Save-the-Wildlife? I mean, if we gonna work here, we don't want that thing in the pit with us, eh?"

"He has a great point, Lynn. How do we get rid of it?" I was just now getting my voice back.

"Where's your phone?"

The cell phone. Of course. I dug it out of my pack and handed it to her.

She called Brian—he had a cell phone, too—and told him what we found. Then she said, "Good. Thank you," and punched it off. "He's coming right over. He has a snake stick, he says."

Only a couple minutes later, a white dust cloud came from beyond the slope. The rising sun and Brian's Jeep arrived at about the same stayed away from it, you didn't try to kill it, and you called for help. I'm proud of you!"

"Where are you gonna take it?" Tiny asked.

"We'll turn it loose down the wash a ways, somewhere well away from where we'll be working." With that boxful of snake venom in his hand—the venom still inside the snake and therefore still dangerous—he walked to his Jeep. Bits and Mike followed.

Lynn and I went back down for the water can. It took two of us to drag that sucker up the hill. I should have thought to ask Tiny and Brian to haul it up; they were both stronger than we were. But my brain was too frizzled.

We put up the shade frame and went to work. It was mindless work, just chipping away, digging all around the little cluster of bones Brian had found. It gave me plenty of time to think.

I thought about how God had helped us out when we didn't even ask Him. We hadn't made all the right moves—the moves Brian praised— because we were so smart or we were used to snakes. I had never seen a rattlesnake before. We made them because—well, because we just did. That, Dad often said, is God's guidance. Dad was big on depending on God for guidance. It had never occurred to me before that he wasn't talking about Sunday school stuff but about everyday stuff.

And I thought about how God whacked us with a rolled-up newspaper, sort of, in order to teach us His lesson. I mean, that was a big

18

Boy, did Dr. Alex Royer ever look grumpy. Not that she ever looked ungrumpy. But today she seemed especially cross. She stood on the cement-block porch in front of her trailer, her fists planted on her hips, and glared at us.

"Us" was Brian and me. We were climbing into the truck to drive into town.

It's not like she wasn't getting any work done. The rest of the gang was already out at V 18 digging for dinosaurs, and the sun wasn't even clear up yet. But Brian and I had to go buy more groceries.

At supper last night she had complained loudly that we were eating her out of house and home. We did not point out that nobody on this dig lived in a house, let alone a home. We just kept our mouths shut, except for apologizing to her.

Brian reminded her that we were also low on plaster and burlap. He made the point that we were running out because we were getting so much done. That was nice of him. We would also return some library books and pick more, because all these were read already.

Dr. Royer did have a point, I suppose. Tiny and Mike and I ate pretty much, and Bits was no slouch, either. Lynn preferred really strange

town sits right on the real Sugar Creek. It has a county park with the river in it. We go there a lot. And we're all Christians except we go to different churches."

"And what's a Christian?"

And the question stopped me cold for a second, because I could tell that he was serious. Somehow the conversation had just turned from light, casual stuff to heavy stuff. "A person who trusts Jesus."

"And tries to do what He wants."

"Sort of . . ." I took a bit to figure out how to say what I wanted to. Even so, it didn't come out as clear as I wished. "But you don't do what He wants so that He'll like you and let you into heaven. You try to do what He wants because He already loves you and did so much for you."

Brian tooled the truck out onto paved road, and the ride smoothed out instantly. "Trying to return the favor?"

"That's not all of it. Trying to please Him just to please Him. Same as I try to please my mom and dad. They love me, so I want to please them. Besides, what they want is the best thing for me, whether I like it or not. Same with Jesus."

"And that's why you kids have your plan to be nice to Dr. Royer."

"Jesus says be good to your enemies." I shrugged. "We'll see."

"You're not going to change anything, you know. She's been this way for as long as I've known her."

some cucumbers, and celery. You know—things you see on those plates of vegetable pieces to dip. "For her," I explained.

When Mom dragged me along grocery shopping, I usually wasn't the least bit interested. But she'd made me learn how to pick out fresh vegetables anyway—how to look for brown edges and wilting and a sort of dry appearance. All of a sudden, that knowledge was coming in pretty handy. You just never know when you're going to use something you thought you'd never need.

We got lots of the big institutional-size cans of stew, chili, and things like that. No cooking, as Brian pointed out with a grin.

Lynn had told me, "Be sure to get a box of spaghetti." And then she reminded me twice. OK, so I got spaghetti. I like the stuff, anyway. I didn't know how much to get, so I chose the two-pound pack of the cheapest brand. Oops, almost forgot the sauce. There were so many different kinds, I had trouble choosing one.

While I went after cereal and sugar, Brian wandered back to the fresh-vegetables aisle again.

We had both carts pretty well filled when we headed for checkout. We'd probably still eat Dr. Royer out of house and home, but this time it would take longer.

When the checker passed a box of fresh white mushrooms across the scanner, Brian looked kind of sheepish, as if he were embarrassed to be buying them. "Might as well, since you got the cauliflower. She likes mushrooms especially."

19

What are just about the biggest, bulkiest bones in your body? Your hip bones—that is, your pelvis. And if you think yours is pretty big, think how big a dinosaur's is.

Brian said that the dinosaur called a tenontosaur got up to twenty or twenty-five feet long. That is one big baby of a pelvis! And the four of us Sugar Creekers were given the job of digging it up. Tiny was off with Brian at V 16, so the rest of us tackled this one.

It was a lot of fun, if you didn't mind plain old raw manual labor. I mean, we dug dirt that was hardened into real rock, although it was very soft rock. You're talking pickaxes here. It was grown-up stuff, and I felt really grown-up doing it.

The pelvis bone, which I would never have recognized, was a foot-long, inch-high crescent of dark gray-brown sticking out of the matrix, the rock around it. When we chipped around it, we found more bone about two inches down, so we had to move out a foot and start chipping from the beginning, all over again, so as to keep the whole bone in one big block. By the time we had reached the edges of the bone group, we had a chunk of matrix three feet wide.

once not too long ago, I had been on the receiving end of one of Bits's rages, and I can tell you, she could blister asphalt. So Dr. Royer was getting as good as she gave.

I didn't know what to do. If I stuck my nose in, would I make the situation better, or would I do harm? What should I say? What could I do? How I wished Tiny or Brian were here! They would know what to do. They were both good at smoothing ruffles.

Then my brain kicked me in the heart. *Well, duh!* it said. *You call yourself a Christian. So trust Jesus, like you told Brian.* So I prayed. It was the only thing I knew to do that would not make this loud, angry scene any worse.

And then, guess who stopped the whole ugly mess dead?

Lynn herself.

"Enough! That's all!" She was always so soft-spoken, I never guessed she could roar so loudly. And she stepped between Bits and Dr. Royer.

Bits paused, looking confused, and even Dr. Royer looked startled.

Lynn shuddered a sigh. "Dr. Royer's right. I did damage. I'm very sorry, ma'am. Bits, we're going to follow the plan. We promised Jesus, and we're going to do it. Please apologize for losing your cool."

Bits turned on her. "But I'm trying to stick up for you!"

"The plan."

"But this isn't . . ." Bits stopped. For a second I thought she couldn't do it. But then she

As soon as Dr. Royer was finished, I laid toilet paper—I mean, paleo paper—on all the exposed fossils and splashed water on it to make it stick.

Bits dumped plaster into a bucket of water and stirred it with her arm. Mike tossed handfuls of long burlap strips into the plaster slurry. He would pull one out and hand it to Lynn. Lynn would lay it on the block. I would pat it down against the rock surface to get rid of bubbles. Lynn would lay down another strip, at an angle. And so on and on until the block was covered.

As we worked, our mood changed from angry and hurtful to happy again. You can't splash around in plaster and stay mad for long. It's too messy and therefore too much fun.

And we were getting pretty good at this jacket business. In just a few minutes, we had the whole block so protected with armor that it could travel the bumpy road back to the university without breaking.

With a big, thick marking pen, Dr. Royer drew the positions of the exposed bones on the surface of the jacket. We cut nearly through the pedestal underneath, rolled the chunk over, and jacketed the top surface.

I sat on the rim of the huge hole we'd dug to watch the top jacket set up. Boy, was I bushed. I swilled the last of the water in my bottle. Bits and Lynn sat down on the rim across from me, their legs dangling into the hole.

And Dr. Royer sat down beside them. This

20

Know how to haul heavy stuff when you're not very strong? By now I was an expert. I was puny, and Mike was small. Bits and Lynn were as strong as eleven year olds get, but that isn't very, when you're faced with a huge chunk of rock like we just jacketed. So we had to resort to tricks.

One good way is to muscle the load onto a blanket or tarp and drag it by the tarp corners. That's how we moved the big block. Another is to roll it. We ended up doing that when the ground got too rough for the tarp. We raised the block to the level of the truck bed by levering it up a ramp made out of a couple of two-by-fours.

You can use two-by-fours as pry bars. One person jams the end of his two-by-four under the block and lifts on the far end. The block moves a wee tiny bit. Beside him, another person wedges her two-by-four under the block and pries up. It moves another inch. But by now it's off the ground and on the ramp, so it's easier to get the pry bars under it.

While we pried, Dr. Royer braced herself up in the truck bed and pulled, hauling on a rope wrapped around the block. There were a whole lot of inches to go up that ramp before

want you to find out what they're planning. They talk to you. You can worm it out of them."

"I really don't think there's anything to worry about, Alex. They—"

"And I'm still sure," she interrupted, "that they have a hand somehow in the thefts. I don't know how they're doing it. They obviously have an accomplice—someone who can drive. But they're doing it."

"Some of the losses occurred when they weren't even here. How could—"

"I said, an accomplice. Think, Brian! They pilfer while they're here and spirit it away by means of the accomplice. The laptop was stolen when they weren't around, so naturally we would not suspect them. Right? It's part of their plot, their means of looking innocent."

A whole computer gone? When they mentioned things turning up missing, I figured they were talking about a shovel, maybe, or a few trowels. But a laptop computer, especially one powerful enough to be used for scientific work, would be top of the line and worth a lot. Grand theft. No small potatoes.

Brian was still trying to get a word in edgewise. "They're harmless, Alex. Even if—"

She interrupted him again. "Haven't you noticed how they're suddenly trying to be nice to me? It's to avert suspicion, Brian. They're bending over backwards to be nice so that I won't tie them to the losses."

"But, Alex—"

"Don't 'but' me! Find out what's going on!"

disappointed that we never saw a Gila monster. A Gila monster (pronounced HE-la, not GUY-la) is a big, beaded lizard, poisonous but not dangerous unless you try to catch it. The Arizona desert (plus a few places in Mexico) is the only place you find them.

But don't feel too sorry for Tiny. He saw all kinds of birds he never saw before, some flowers, different kinds of cactus, and a bunch of lizards, so he didn't do too badly as a naturalist.

With four of us and Brian all working V 16, we dug out two little ribs in no time at all. The pieces were small—maybe a foot to fifteen inches —so we jacketed them, not with burlap dipped in plaster, but with instant medical casts. You wrap a long, treated strip around the piece and get it wet. Almost instantly, it turns into a cast. If you broke your arm, the doctor would use one. We used them when we didn't want to mix a big batch of plaster for a little job.

I told the others what I'd heard, but I didn't mention anything to Brian. He already knew about our plan. Either he didn't connect it to the "plot" Dr. Royer was so worried about, or he realized what was going on and kept his mouth shut.

But being accused of ripping off a laptop angered me. That's serious.

We carried our prizes down to the Jeep.

"How do you know where to dig?" I asked Brian. "You've got the whole state of Arizona to search in. Why do you look here and not somewhere else?"

I had ridden all over Buck's land on that horse, inhaling dust. But I hadn't noticed that the rocks there were not the same as these. On the other hand, now that Brian explained it, I did remember a difference, sort of.

Because this was going to be a small, fast job, we hadn't brought lunch. So we climbed into the Jeep and headed back to camp for the important stuff. Food.

We had just gotten back when Tiny and Dr. Royer returned. I finished smearing sunscreen on my face as I walked out to their truck. The plaster fossil jackets had been replaced by plastic grocery sacks.

I grabbed a sack in each hand and headed for Dr. Royer's trailer without being asked. Right behind me, Mike took two more. Lynn carried in two bags of fresh vegetables. Then she stayed inside with Dr. Royer, helping to wash them and cut them up.

I'm going to be a world-famous chef someday, if I don't become a paleontologist first, so I stayed and helped, too.

Mom had taught me how to chop vegetables without losing fingers. First, you use the right kind of knife, one with a very broad blade. Next, when you hold steady the carrot or whatever with one hand, you curl your fingers under, so that your knuckles stick out beyond the rest. They are up high enough that they stay beside the broad knife blade instead of under it. So you can rock the knife back and forth and chop like sixty and stay in one piece.

vice? He's Canadian. "'A bunch of the boys were whooping it up . . .'?"

"No." And Dr. Royer's voice sounded as cold as Canadian tundra.

"Oh." Lynn sounded disappointed. "None at all?"

Tiny appeared in the doorway, so I handed him a plate of veggies. We gathered up the sandwich fixings and headed outside.

Dr. Royer, as usual, stayed behind and ate in the trailer, catching up on her e-mail while she munched raw veggies. The rest of us dined on bologna out at the picnic table.

Brian had rigged the table with a big shade umbrella. It made lunch a lot more comfortable.

Afterwards, Brian headed off to the other trailer to do something—I don't know what—and the five of us cleaned up the lunch mess. A dish towel draped over her shoulder, Lynn went over to the water wagon for water to rinse out the glasses.

I ran after her. "Hey, Lynn? Wait up!"

She cranked the spigot. Water slammed into the bucket, drumming on the bottom.

"What was that all about?" I asked.

"What was what all about?" She turned it off.

"Canadian poetry."

"You got spaghetti like I asked, didn't you?"

"Yeah. But we're talking about poetry."

Lynn handed me the dish towel. "My father likes Robert Service's poetry. He has several books of it."

22

Two days to go, today and tomorrow. The time had gone fast. Our stack of new library books was read and reread. The Monopoly game was about worn out. Time to go.

I felt sad. Isn't that nuts? We were hot and sweaty and uncomfortable most of the time. We worked like slaves. And I was sorry to see it end. Even the rattly old generator was getting to feel like a familiar and welcome old friend.

Brian made us all bacon and eggs for breakfast. Lynn and I helped serve. We drank extra orange juice, leaving only enough for tomorrow, so that we'd have less food to take back.

Dr. Royer seemed more at ease this morning. She didn't smile—I doubted her mouth was able to turn up at the corners—but she acted more relaxed. She even ate out at the picnic table with the rest of us.

Brian finished his toast. "Alex? Remember the old saying?"

"Which one?"

"The last day of a dig is when you make the really great find."

She smirked. "That's always the way it goes."

Then we climbed into the crew-cab truck

popped out of a nearby palo verde and flitted away. I had no idea what it was.

I saw that erosion had cut through several layers of earth. I recognized the gray that we always had to dig down through, the overburden. And then there ran a layer of white dinosaur stratum. I followed it by eye as it ran along the hillside, but I didn't see any dinosaur color in it.

I did see a patch of strange gray in it, though. I figured that the layer above had somehow washed down into a crack, filling it. I went over to look closer.

The patch was too crusty and light to be dinosaur. Or was it? I found a dry stick and poked at it a little. I poked more. I noticed that the gravel I knelt in had lots of tiny chips that looked like fossil bits.

When I straightened up and looked around, I saw another patch of that crusty gray. And another and . . . the whole white layer was riddled with gray patches. And one of them included the shiny dark gray of a dinosaur tooth! I splacked my hat down on the find and ran back around the hill.

"Brian! Hey, Brian! Dr. Royer! Come!"

"Now what?" Dr. Royer said crossly.

Brian, though, dropped the notebook he was writing in and headed my way.

"I think I found something! Come see!" And I ran back around the hill. I was too excited to just walk, because if this was what I thought it was . . .

23

It amazes me the way people change when they get excited. Mike, for instance, would bob up and down. "Bounces off the walls," his brother put it. Bits bounced off walls, too, but she'd also start talking nonstop. Brian grinned so widely you could slide a dinner plate into his mouth without touching teeth. And Dr. Royer got intense and serious.

Now, you might argue that Dr. Royer was never not serious. True. I mean, more serious. Much more serious and more intense. Not grim so much as . . . focused. That's it. Focused.

She stood up and yanked her cell phone off her belt. She listened, scowled, poked in numbers, listened some more, scowled harder. "We're going to have to go back to camp. I can't get out from here."

"Who are you going to call?" Bits had joined us.

"I have to teach a summer-school session starting Monday. Your fathers are coming to get you tomorrow. But possibly some of our paleo graduate students have come back for school." She looked at Brian. "If I can get Bobbi or Rick out here, we can retrieve some of this material over the weekend. Enough to figure out what we have."

so cool!" And he dropped down to start working on a big patch.

Lynn clapped her hands eagerly. "Let's go, Bits!"

Tiny and I beat Dr. Royer back to the truck. We hopped in the back, she torched it off, and we bucketed out of there a lot faster than usual. It was a wild ride to the camp, with a lot of lurching and bouncing. Dr. Royer could drive like a NASCAR pro.

We pulled into the dusty yard, and she hit the brakes so hard we skidded a little bit. Yeah! Tiny and I jumped out.

Dr. Royer slammed her door. "You two get that unopened bag of plaster and fill the two spare water cans. We'll need more shovels, too."

"Dr. Royer?" I raised a hand.

She paused. "What?"

"The generator."

"I don't hear the . . ." She drew a deep breath.

Exactly. The yard was silent. They always left the generator on to power the fridge and swamp coolers. It wasn't running now.

Instantly furious, she stomped around behind the trailer toward the bushes. "I told Brian to refuel it last night! I told him! Why can't he . . ." And she stopped cold.

Tiny and I stepped up beside her.

The generator was gone. There was the cement pad it had been bolted to. There was the cut-off end of the power line leading to the trailers. Its copper gleamed bright and shiny in the sun.

"You know what?" I said. "Our dads would love to help. Let me try to call them. Maybe they can come back early and give us a hand."

But I couldn't raise them. Either they were away from the cell phone or out of satellite contact.

Then we all headed back out to V 18.

A generator missing. If something like a shovel or trowel is missing, you figure you just laid it down someplace and lost it. Maybe even a laptop. But you don't misplace a generator.

Tiny was thinking, too. I could tell, because he stared out at the space beyond the windshield.

I used some of the time to pray. And high time, too. Too much was happening too fast.

Then, as happens sometimes when I pray, my mind started to wander. And suddenly, for no reason, a light dawned. I wish I could say I sorted through all the clues and arrived at the solution to the crime. But no. One moment it wasn't in my head, and the next moment it was there. I knew who the thief was.

"Thought you wasn't gonna call me 'sir.' Howdy, Alex. Come on out to the sun porch. I'll have Maria fetch us up some iced tea and—"

"I'd rather visit in the living room."

"It's . . . uh . . . ain't been cleaned yet." Buck frowned at me.

"Les says you have some very nice fossils on your mantel."

"Well, yeah." He stared at me harder.

Dr. Royer kept talking. "With dinosaur specimens. There are no terrestrial strata on your land. It's all marine. If you have dinosaur material, it came from somewhere other than your property. The university's dig, perhaps?"

"Where I get my stuff ain't none of your concern." He scowled at me now. "Les, you telling stories about me?"

"No, sir. But I remembered Brian said you don't have any dinosaur layers, and there were dinosaur pieces on your mantel along with the shark teeth and stuff. I thought maybe you wouldn't invite the university people into your living room because you were afraid they might notice. But you didn't think we kids were smart enough to."

"That's crazy. I'm ashamed of you, Les."

I continued, "And you were the only one around when Bits and I found that tooth. It would have been easy for you to go back as soon as we left and dig the jaw out. Mike saw your horse's tracks. We thought it was when you stopped by the first time, but you didn't ride in that close when we were there. And

rassment, it appeared, but with anger. "I'm gonna get off scot-free on this, and you know it! You're such a witch, nobody's gonna take your side. So you lost a couple little things. Who cares? You deserve it!"

I couldn't believe this. "Buck, you mean you think it's OK to steal as long as you don't like the person you're stealing from?"

"You ain't no dumb kid, Les. How do you like working for her? You gonna tell me she's nice?"

"No, sir. But she's honest. She doesn't like kids much. But she's honest about that, too. She doesn't lie or pretend. And she cares very much about what she's doing."

The dust cloud was not one sheriff's vehicle, but two—a sedan and a pickup. The truck parked by Dr. Royer's truck. The sedan whipped on down to the bunkhouse and stopped square in front of Buck's pickup, blocking it. Two deputies jumped out. I saw Manny slowly get out of Buck's vehicle.

The two deputies in the truck here by the house got out and came striding toward us. They were as grim as Dr. Royer ever got.

The anger in Buck's face melted into fear, then anger again. "You ain't getting away with this, Miz Sourpuss! You'll see!"

The two deputies down by the bunkhouse radioed up to the two beside us. In the back of Buck's pickup was a generator, they said. Its power line was hacked off as if it had been moved in a hurry. The deputy added, "It has to be worth a couple thou, at least."

anything. Dad claimed that was always a good thing to do.

Then her voice softened. "I'm jealous of Brian, in a way. He gets along so comfortably with all of you. I suppose I'm especially jealous about the practical joking."

"You mean like the teeth?"

"Exactly. Mike said, 'Look! I found meat-eater teeth!' And it turned out that he'd secretly buried them. Snaggle teeth, the kind you wear at Halloween. It was a good, harmless joke. And Brian was still laughing about it a day later."

I smiled at the thought. "Mike comes by teasing naturally. His brothers are all practical jokers. He brought some other fun things with him besides the teeth. There's a glass that dribbles when you try to drink from it. Stuff like that."

She nodded. "No one has ever tried a practical joke on me. Not once."

"Really? Wow!"

"I think that's what I envy most. The lack of . . . camaraderie. Do you know what that is?"

"No, ma'am."

She studied the steering wheel a moment. "It means being comfortable in each other's company. Teasing and jokes are part of it, but it's more than that. It's friendship, too. Warmth. I've never known that." She fell silent.

It seemed time to change the subject. After a minute, I said, "This dinosaur we're digging up now. It really is something rare?"

"This is especially good luck," Brian said. "If this wash had eroded for another year, all this would have been carried away."

I wondered how much of the past was already gone—ground up to make sand on the seashore someplace.

That night we all ate supper together—a really late supper, because we'd worked so long. Yep, even Dr. Royer ate with us. Not only that, she ate canned chili. But then, it was great chili. I added onion and the last of the celery, chopped fine. Lynn ladled the chili from the pan into bowls. She'd hand the bowls to me, and I'd dump plenty of grated cheese on top before passing them on to the diners. Maybe you can't exactly call canned chili "fine dining," but it sure seemed that way.

Toward the end of the meal, Mike took the empty pitcher over to the wagon and refilled it. He sat down again and poured himself another glass of water. We were all drinking many glasses of water, tossing in ice cubes now and then just to take the heat off.

Mike peered down into his glass. "Boy, our ice sure melts fast, doesn't it? Hey, look! An ice worm!"

The other four of us kids jumped up and shouldered each other aside some, trying to get a good look in his glass.

"Wow!" said Tiny. "That's great. You never find one in city water. It's too chlorinated."

"Neat," Lynn added.